Santa Claus

and the

Law of Attraction

A Christmas Story for the Believer in All of Us

Celeste Eckman Himanek

Balboa Press books may be ordered through booksellers or by contacting:

Balboa Press
A Division of Hay House
1663 Liberty Drive
Bloomington, IN 47403
www.balboapress.com
1 (877) 407-4847

Design by Deborah Perdue, Illumination Graphics
Custom illustrations by Tara Thelen and Ariel Himanek
Thanks to deposit.photos.com and shutterstock.com

First Edition
Printed in U.S.A.

ISBN: 978-1-9822-3600-7 (sc)
ISBN: 978-1-9822-3601-4 (e)

Library of Congress Control Number: 2019915352

Print information available on the last page.

Balboa Press rev. date: 10/07/2019

BALBOA
PRESS
A DIVISION OF HAY HOUSE

Dedication

This book is dedicated to
my grandmother, Bernice,
my mother, Beverly,
and my mother-in-law, Betty,
who brought the love for
all things Christmas into our lives
and taught us how to believe.
And also to Jim and Ariel:
Thank you for helping me make this dream come true.
You make every day Christmas. I love you.

T'was the night before Christmas
and all through the house,
not a creature was stirring
and I felt like a louse.

I was tossing and turning;
I just couldn't sleep.
I was worried about money.
We were in debt so deep.

The children were nestled
all snug in their beds,
but not dreaming of sugar plums
like the old book said.

My oldest one wanted
just one thing: a bike.
It was just so much cheaper
when she rode a trike.

The younger one's hooked
on video games already.
Can we have back the days
when he just wanted a stuffed teddy?

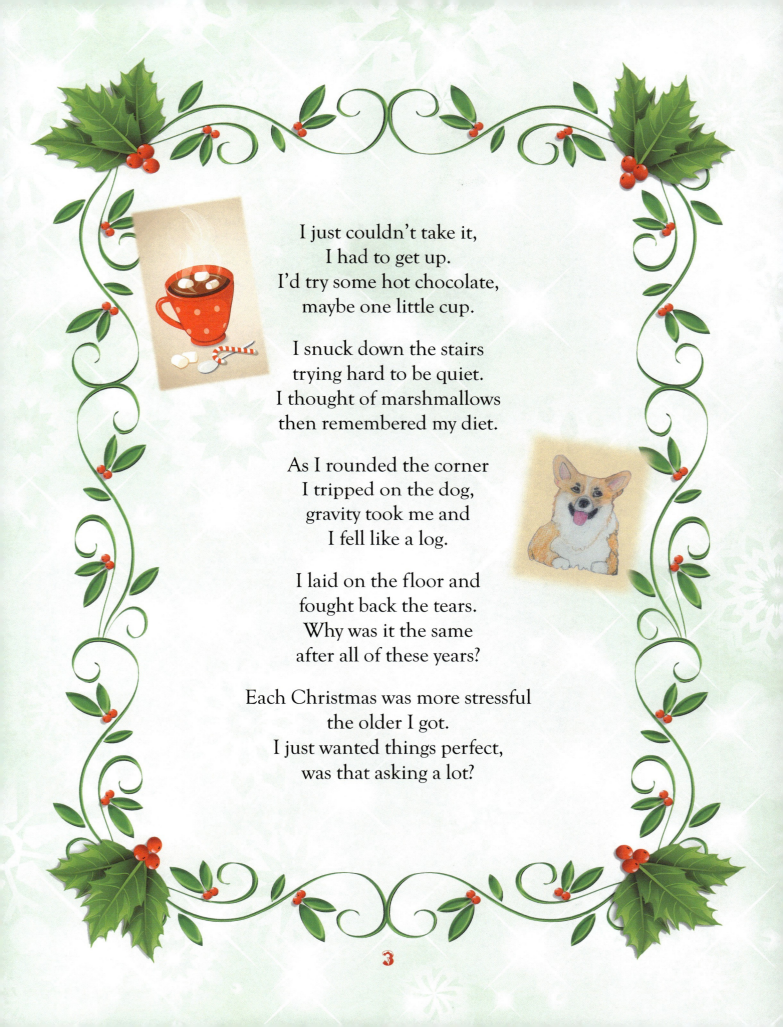

I just couldn't take it,
I had to get up.
I'd try some hot chocolate,
maybe one little cup.

I snuck down the stairs
trying hard to be quiet.
I thought of marshmallows
then remembered my diet.

As I rounded the corner
I tripped on the dog,
gravity took me and
I fell like a log.

I laid on the floor and
fought back the tears.
Why was it the same
after all of these years?

Each Christmas was more stressful
the older I got.
I just wanted things perfect,
was that asking a lot?

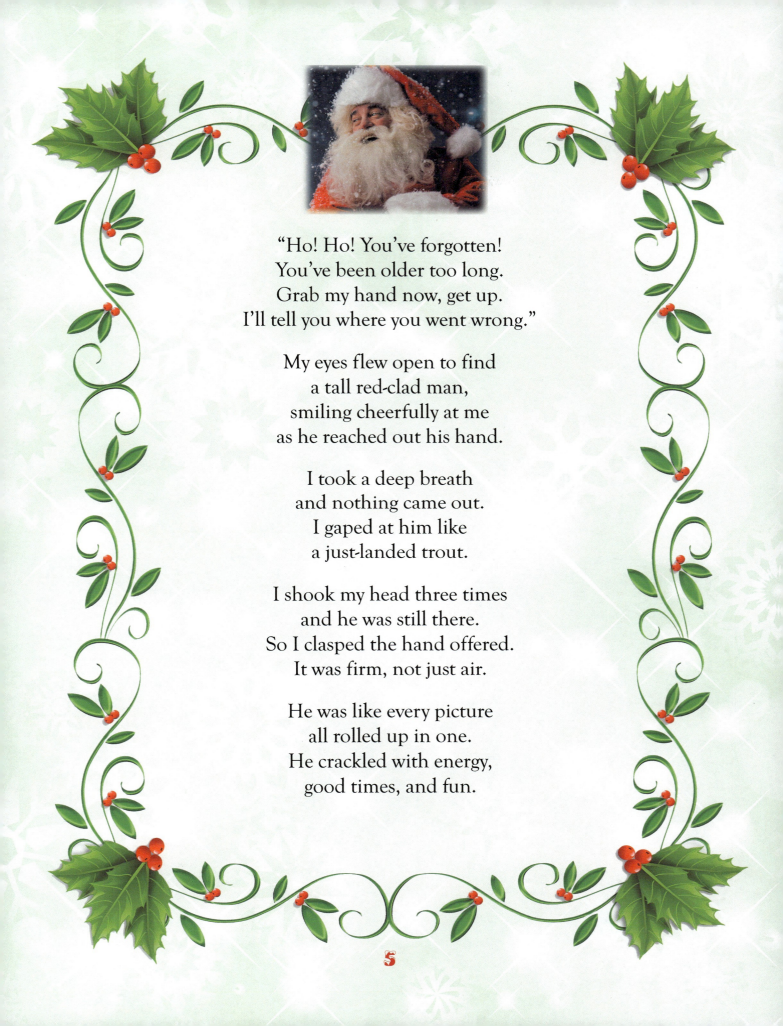

"Ho! Ho! You've forgotten!
You've been older too long.
Grab my hand now, get up.
I'll tell you where you went wrong."

My eyes flew open to find
a tall red-clad man,
smiling cheerfully at me
as he reached out his hand.

I took a deep breath
and nothing came out.
I gaped at him like
a just-landed trout.

I shook my head three times
and he was still there.
So I clasped the hand offered.
It was firm, not just air.

He was like every picture
all rolled up in one.
He crackled with energy,
good times, and fun.

I looked into his eyes
so brilliant, so blue.
My voice came back as
I breathed out, "You're true."

"You've forgotten the magic
of how these things go.
As a child you believed,
you just went with the flow.

You wrote out your list
of all that you wanted.
The price didn't matter,
your faith was undaunted.

You put it on paper,
and set your intention.
No detail was too small
for you not to mention.

You waited with joy
and great expectation,
then brought it to life
with your visualizations.

You could see it and feel it
and knew it by heart.
Whatever you asked for
you knew every part.

You knew you deserved it.
You'd been good and believed,
so you felt the excitement
and knew you'd receive.

You got what you wanted
more often than not.
The universe answered
when it heard you knock.

The Polar Express,
The Santa Clause, and more.
And that one with the girl
Down on Street 34?

Those movies you love?
They all say the same:
believe to achieve
is the name of the game.

Kids ask and they write
and believe that it's theirs.
They know they deserve it
when they say their prayers.

The magic is there
every day of the year,
but you must be real careful
the Universe also hears fear.

Your worries are like praying
for all that you lack.
That's why things stay the same
and they keep coming back.

You ask, then you doubt.
Like planting seeds, then don't water.
It's like being on a giant
Law of Attraction teeter-totter.

You believe, then you don't
and then you lose focus,
start doubting the magic
and think it's all hocus-pocus.

You read Louise Hay!
Wayne Dyer and Chopra!
Bob Proctor! Jack Canfield!
And Lisa and Oprah!

You've listened to Abraham
Through Esther and Jerry.
You want things so much
but your vibration's not merry.

Your inbox is full
of webinars and sessions
on hypnosis, brain entrainment,
intuition, and tapping lessons.

You're full of distress
that you might miss a Secret.
Should you meditate with Dispenza?
Return Quantum Jumping or keep it?

By all means enjoy
all that brain stuff and physics,
but reading's not doing
the real work now, is it?

I'm afraid you've become
an LOA junkie, my dear.
Time to get back to basics,
shut the door on your fear.

You've got all the pieces,
now enjoy the puzzle.
Try to see it as fun,
not an endless struggle."

"But my kids depend on me!
It's so hard to relax.
How can I not worry
or forget my lack?"

"The energy flows
where the attention goes.
You need to think good thoughts,
though it's hard, heaven knows."

"That sounds so simplistic,
so easy, so trite.
Don't worry about money
when I can't sleep at night?"

He laughed again softly,
and patted my head.
He looked at me kindly
And here's what he said:

"It is just that simple, my dear.
Can't you see?
It's simple, not easy,
but take it from me.

Your thoughts become things
and that is your magic.
It's when you forget
that things turn tragic.

The world is so busy
it makes you forget
that the Source is inside you.
It's your safety net.

You've been looking outside
yourself with every turn.
The answer's inside you,
this you must learn.

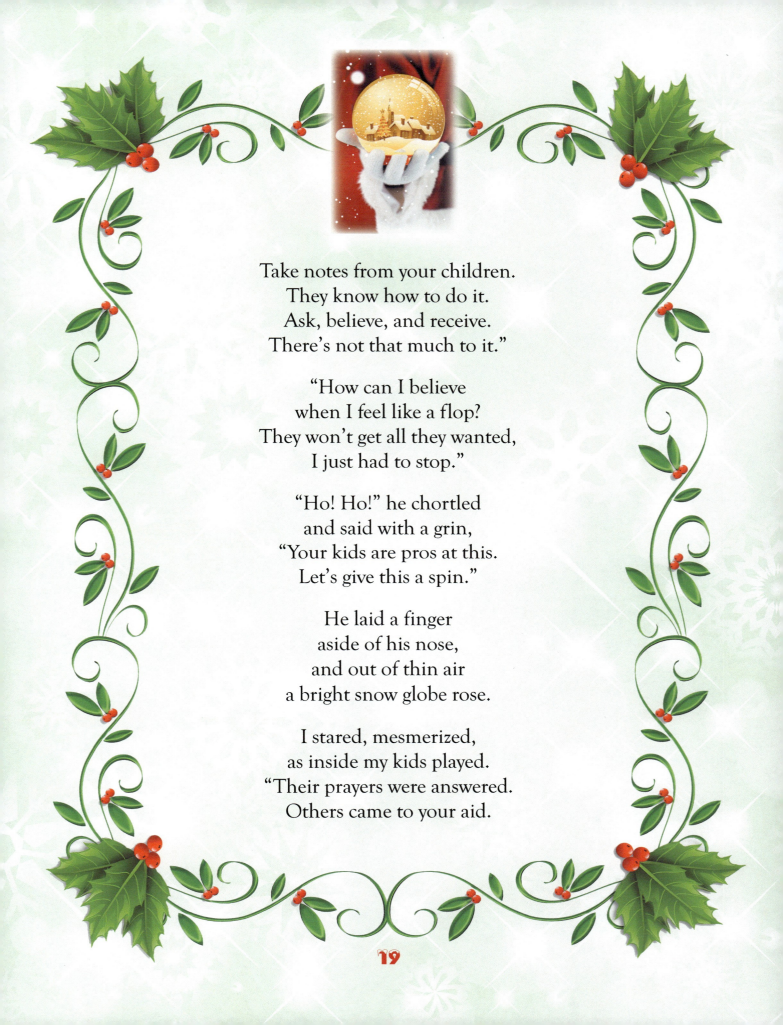

Take notes from your children.
They know how to do it.
Ask, believe, and receive.
There's not that much to it."

"How can I believe
when I feel like a flop?
They won't get all they wanted,
I just had to stop."

"Ho! Ho!" he chortled
and said with a grin,
"Your kids are pros at this.
Let's give this a spin."

He laid a finger
aside of his nose,
and out of thin air
a bright snow globe rose.

I stared, mesmerized,
as inside my kids played.
"Their prayers were answered.
Others came to your aid.

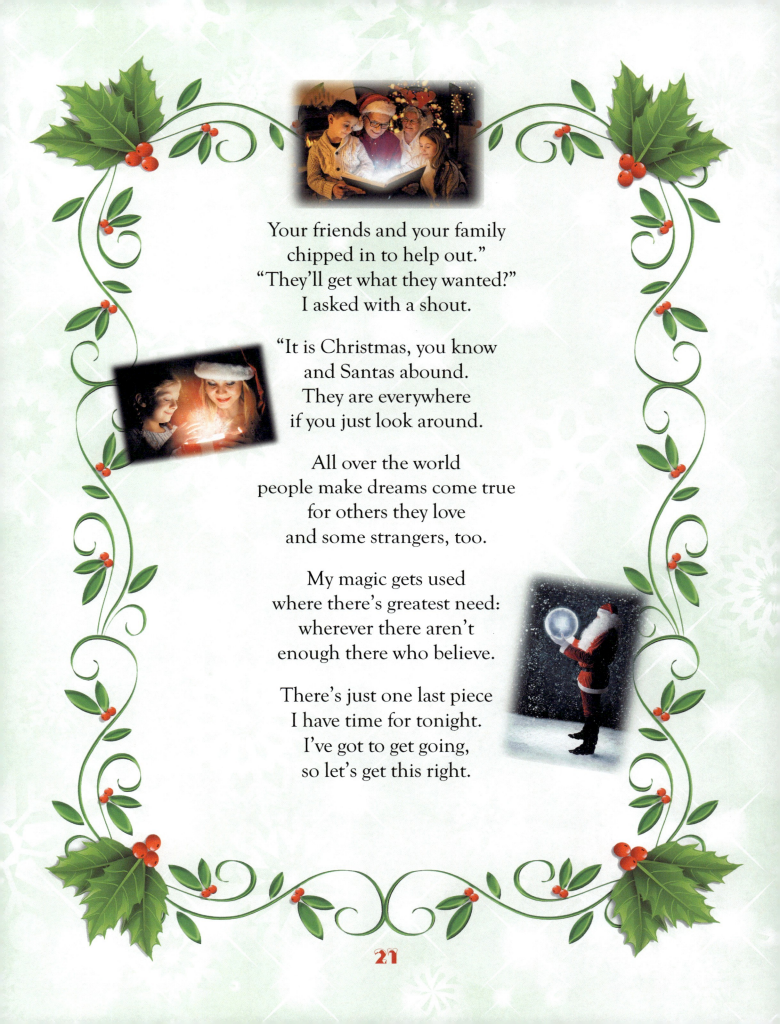

Your friends and your family
chipped in to help out."
"They'll get what they wanted?"
I asked with a shout.

"It is Christmas, you know
and Santas abound.
They are everywhere
if you just look around.

All over the world
people make dreams come true
for others they love
and some strangers, too.

My magic gets used
where there's greatest need:
wherever there aren't
enough there who believe.

There's just one last piece
I have time for tonight.
I've got to get going,
so let's get this right.

What else keeps you from getting
those things you want now,
is you get yourself knackered
worrying about how.

How will it happen?
How can it be?
Are the ways and the means
all left up to me?

No, how's not up to you,
like that girl sings in Frozen,
'Let it go!' after you ask,
then you'll get what you've chosen.

You also might find
when your blessings arrive,
that they are even better
than you dared to contrive.

Now I really must go,
it's my busiest night.
My reindeer are restless
to resume their flight."

"How can I thank you
for all that you've done?
You've given me hope again
When before I had none."

He sighed, and he touched my cheek
with his glove,
and my heart just about
exploded with love.

"You've believed in me
all of your life, so I came.
I wanted to help you
learn to win at this game.

Life is meant to be joyous,
and loving, and fun.
when you figure that out,
then that's when you've won.

Please thank me by living
your life with more joy,
and seeing it's more
about love than the toys.

Be nice to yourself,
you're still on my list.
I'll be watching," he said,
then gave me a kiss.

He was gone in a blink,
as it started snowing.
And suddenly I was
graced with a knowing.

I'd believed in him always
and he came through for me.
Santa helped me remember:
The best gift is in me.

The Story Behind the Story

Cover artwork by Leonard Weisgard from *The Night Before Christmas*

I don't know about you, but I have always been a "Why?" child. Why is the sky blue? Why do I have to _____? Fill in the blank. I asked that one a lot. I often drove my Grandmother to the brink of exasperation. Anyway, I always like to know the stories behind the story and knowing the meaning helps me to have a greater understanding of things, especially if I want to try something for myself. In case you're like me, here are the stories behind the story.

The poem made famous by Clement C. Moore is one of the elements that inspired this book. After I had my daughter in 2004, I wanted to make sure that the edition of *The Night Before Christmas* she grew up with would be the same as the one I remembered.

Illustrated by the famed Leonard Weisgard, the cover is awash in blue-green; the snow has fallen and a full moon glows in the winter night, visible just under a pine branch. Santa is flying low over a church and the surrounding houses, jauntily waving as his reindeer pull him forward to the next rooftop.

My daughter was born in June, and when Christmas rolled around I was thrilled to find the right copy. My mother read this to me every year on Christmas Eve, and on many other nights during the Christmas season. My mother is a gifted speaker; her voice is warm, her delivery is animated, and she brought the words to life for me with every reading. I felt like I was in that story when she read it to me. When Papa sprang from his bed to see what was the matter, I almost jumped out of mine with him. When she softly whispered about the moon on the breast of the new-fallen snow, I held my breath so I could hear what was coming next (although I already knew). Her voice would pick up speed and intensity as he was whistling and shouting and calling them by name: "Now, Dasher! now, Dancer! now, Prancer and Vixen! On, Comet! on, Cupid! on Donder and Blixen! To the top of the porch! to the top of the wall! Now dash away! dash away! dash away, all!" Her voice was full of mirth as she described St. Nick, and as she told about him rising up the chimney she would lay her finger aside my own nose. She would exclaim "Happy Christmas to all and to all a Good Night!" as the book came to an end and then snap the book shut.

My mother has always loved Christmas, just like her mother before her. I was raised to believe in Santa and that was never in contradiction to my Catholic upbringing. Both existed in my world; there was no either or for me. It is my great good luck that my husband is also a Santa believer who comes from a family of Christmas lovers. I now see that one's standing on the matter of Christmas is very important selection criteria when choosing a life partner. So, as my daughter neared her first Christmas, he shared in my desire to make it magical and memorable. I found the book and he carved her very first Christmas ornament to match the angel found inside the cover. Thus began one of our own family traditions, and that angel will be part of every Christmas. Interestingly enough, the original copyright for this version of the book is 1949. It was released again in 2004, the year my daughter was born.

Inside illustration by Leonard Weisgard from *The Night Before Christmas*
and my husband's hand-carved Christmas ornament for our daughter's first Christmas

The other inspiration for this book was not the lifetime of good Christmases I have had, but two truly awful ones.

The first truly awful one was back in the 80s. I was working for a lovely family-owned business that had always been incredibly generous with bonuses at Christmas time. I loved working for them for many reasons, and must admit this was one of them. It really made my Christmas shopping more fun.

My method of Christmas shopping at that point in my life was more like aerobic exercise. It lasted all day and I must have burned a ton of calories. Dashing through the aisles, my feeling was not one of stress, but rather one of love and exhilaration. I had my list, I knew what I wanted, and I knew where I was going to get it. I almost always found exactly what I was looking for. And when I got my hands on it, I would be so excited about how the giftee was going to love it, I would almost chortle with glee like some crazed overgrown elf. Really. I loved shopping like that. I always went alone and I had a blast. Did I mention that it was always just before Christmas? And I do mean JUST. It depended on when I got paid and when I got that amazing, generous bonus. That bonus let me feel like Santa, and I didn't have to worry about anything.

My shopping was totally infused with serious gratitude. I would kiss that check on the way to the bank (this was way before direct deposit) and say thank you, thank you, thank you all the way there. I would be so jazzed because this whole day was full of so many things I loved best: all the Christmas decorations, the music in the air, the snow (I lived in Michigan most of my life, so there was almost always snow), the lights, Santa, and people being a little bit nicer to each other.

I got to spend my time thinking about the people I loved, how much fun it was to buy them what I hoped they would like, and imagining their faces when they got it. I always bought myself a new book in the morning since I knew I would be standing in line throughout the day and would have time to read in line, at lunch, and at dinner at the end of my spree. Pure bliss. Christmas shopping day was always one of my most wonderful days of the year. Until the year that it wasn't.

One year, Ebenezer Scrooge entered the stage and ruined my Christmas. Ebenezer showed up in the form of an accountant who advised the lovely family I worked for that it made more fiscal sense to give those bonuses after the start of the New Year. I find it difficult to convey the sense of absolute, total dread that fell over me when I found out. I also felt physically ill. What was I going to do without that money? I felt choked up, embarrassed, and stupid that I had placed all my Christmas eggs in one basket. How could I be so dumb? Why hadn't I planned ahead? I wasn't very financially intelligent at that point. I was pretty young and this was one of my first "real" jobs. They had set the Christmas bonus precedent and I had worked there for a few years when this happened. I had been lulled into a kind of Christmas complacency. It was devastating and I truly felt ashamed. I felt like I should have known better.

It took me a day or two to recover from the shock. And then determination set in. I wasn't going to let that damn Grinch . . . or Scrooge . . . steal my Christmas. No flipping way. I borrowed enough money from a family friend to let me feel like Santa again, and off I went. Money, or the lack of it, wouldn't stop Christmas from coming that year. I kissed that money with gratitude, and hugged and kissed the friend with gratitude, too. A lot. And then I went shopping.

My shopping was not as deliciously joyous

that year. I had suffered a loss. It really felt like the death of my Christmas innocence, but I was grimly determined to enjoy my Christmas anyway. No longer a Christmas virgin, so to speak, what rose up in place of that innocence was my intention. I created that happiness on purpose. I took stock of what I needed to pull it off and I did it. It was about more than the money, of course, but that helped. And I later paid off the family friend. Every penny.

I learned a lot that year. I learned that I never wanted to feel that way again: blindsided, lacking, foolish, and even desperate. It really broke my heart a little.

I'd like to say that I then became a well-organized woman who always had her shopping done by September or some other warm-weather month. But no. I had established some warped Christmas habits that had been in place for too many years. I got better about handling my money, too, but my Christmas karma deemed it necessary that I have one more Christmas disaster astoundingly similar to the one I mentioned earlier, this time in 2011. Again, I had a large sum due to arrive in early December and again, it didn't. Ouch. And yes, it hurt worse this time because a) now I really did know better and b) now I had a husband and daughter to buy for, too. I was truly ashamed that I had let this happen again. The self-recrimination was strong in this one (me), as you can well imagine. As Pema Chodron says, "Nothing ever goes away until it has taught us what we need to know . . . " Chodron has also said, "Rather than letting our negativity get the better of us, we could acknowledge that right now we feel like a piece of shit and not be squeamish about taking a good look." I absolutely felt like excrement, and this time, I took a better look at what the heck I was doing.

As my life had gotten more complicated with the addition of a husband, a daughter, grad school, and work, I hadn't made any accommodations for doing things any better or smarter. I just got overwhelmed and tried to keep doing them the way I always had. And as Zig Ziglar used to say, "If you keep doing what you've been doing, you're gonna keep getting what you've been getting." I definitely did not want any more of this crap. I had had enough.

I learned to start sooner. I started to put dates on my calendar for when I wanted things done. Tree up by this date, presents wrapped by this date, Christmas cards sent by this date. Well, okay. I still stink at getting cards sent. But I am much better at the rest. Online shopping has really been a blessing for me. Thank you, God, for Amazon. I start months ahead of time and I order things as I see them, no matter what time of year it is. And spreading the cost out over months is much easier on me, too. My only challenge is finding them later in the year after squirrelling them away all summer where no one, including me, will find them by accident. I've learned that doing this Christmas stuff ahead of time is really a way of being nice to myself. Less stress, less worry, and less chance for disaster. I did still forget some things last year, but at least this time it wasn't big enough to qualify as a disaster, just a good face-palm or two.

As you may have guessed by now, the emotions in the poem are real. And the Law of Attraction (LOA) stuff? I'm a believer. Are you?

In case you don't know what it is, at lawofattraction.com, they define it this way: "Simply put, the Law of Attraction is the ability to attract into our lives whatever we are focusing on. It is believed that regardless of age, nationality or religious belief, we are all susceptible to the laws which govern the Universe, including the Law of Attraction. It is the Law of Attraction which uses the power of the mind to translate whatever is in our thoughts and materialize them into reality. In basic terms, **all thoughts turn into things eventually**. If you focus on negative doom and gloom you will remain under that cloud. If you focus on positive thoughts and have goals that you aim to achieve you will find a way to achieve them with massive action. This is why the universe is such an infinitely beautiful place. The Law of Attraction dictates that whatever can be imagined and held in the mind's eye is achievable if you take action on a plan to get to where you want to be."

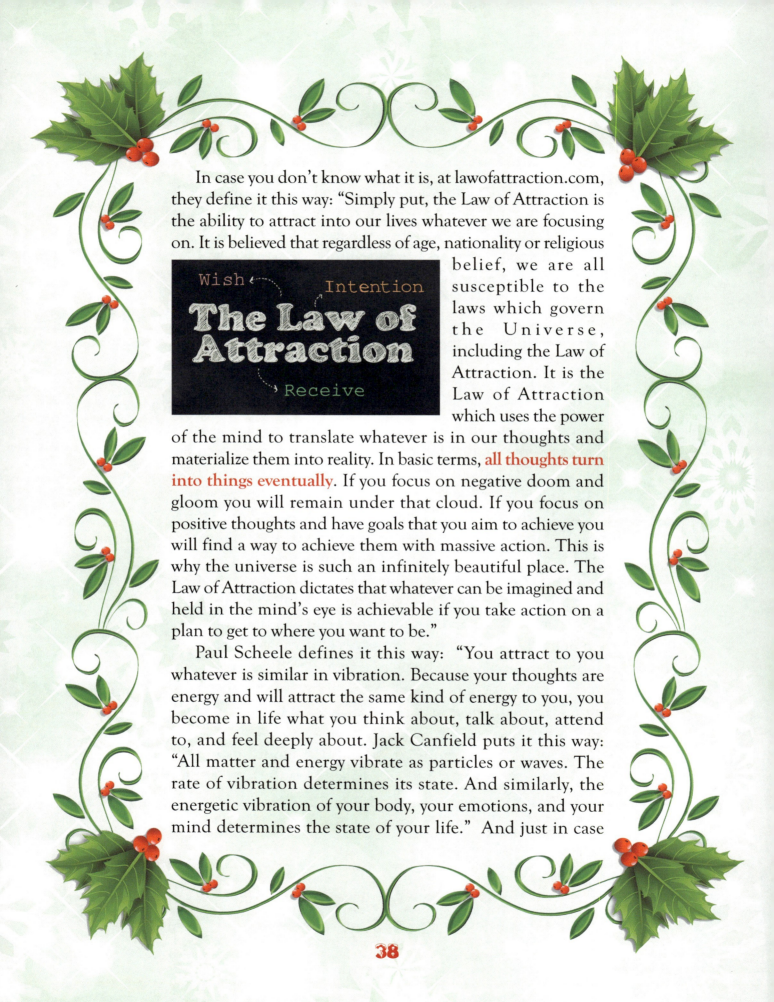

Paul Scheele defines it this way: "You attract to you whatever is similar in vibration. Because your thoughts are energy and will attract the same kind of energy to you, you become in life what you think about, talk about, attend to, and feel deeply about. Jack Canfield puts it this way: "All matter and energy vibrate as particles or waves. The rate of vibration determines its state. And similarly, the energetic vibration of your body, your emotions, and your mind determines the state of your life." And just in case

you think this sounds too far out or "woo woo," science supports this.

Today, a search for Law of Attraction on Google yielded "about 1,000,000 search results" and a previous search on Amazon showed 19,604 results. It really is a thing.

Since it's not about sitting on the sofa and just wishing for stuff, what is it? How do thoughts become things?

I can't remember **exactly** when I started getting interested in the LOA stuff, but sometime in 2006 I remember being introduced to the movie *What the Bleep do We Know*, which was released in 2004. It is aptly described as a "hard to describe movie" that is a mix of science and spirituality, story and documentary, and it introduced me to the wacky world of Quantum Physics. I seriously love science, so I was in. Then the movie *The Secret* burst upon the scene in 2006, and was wildly popular. I found the movie tough to watch as it made it seem like you just had to stand in front of a store window and gaze longingly at what you want and POOF! it would be yours. It seemed too materialistic, and I turned it off pretty quickly. But I did end up listening to the book since a friend kept insisting that I needed to. It got more interesting. Then I went back and watched the movie. I started to find this stuff compelling and started sucking it up all up in earnest around 2012ish. I was intrigued by the science, warmed by the spiritual aspects, and motivated to master it by my desire for a more financially secure future. So I started to study it. I won't say that I've mastered it, but I have had some brilliant moments that inspire me to keep at it. The more I learn, the more it makes sense to me. What was really fun for me was when I looked back at some of the moments in my life that I thought were absolutely magical. Had I created those magical happenings? I always thought I was magic when I was a kid, because good things that I really wanted seemed to happen for me. Let me tell you about my first truly magical happening.

I am a writer. From my earliest memory of, "What do you want to be when you grow up?" my answer was always, "A writer." Later I would add many things, since none of us are just one thing. Next was horse trainer, then jockey, then rider on the Olympic Equestrian Team (when I grew too tall to be a jockey), then a doctor (unsure what kind, but had to make money to support those horses), then a counselor  (yes, that kind of doctor), and also a motivational speaker (now they call them transformational). But always a writer. I won my first writing award in 7th grade for something I wrote about horses (the topic was not a big surprise, the award was).

I remember being lectured by one of my teachers that I needed to broaden my horizons because all I read about was horses. That was her response when I had read every horse book in the school library and complained to her when I found out *The Yearling* was about a deer. Not only was it about a deer and not a horse, but the whole book seemed pretty dreadful to me. I skimmed it when I found out it wasn't a horse story, something I would never do otherwise. I am not one of those book cheaters who read the end. Or not very often, anyway. But back to *The Yearling.* It still seems pretty dreadful, and widely acclaimed or not I refuse to read it. Why? Because it's sad and even at that early age I didn't want to read about things that dragged me down or made me sad. At this no-longer-a –spring-chicken age, I still don't want to read things that drag me down or make me sad. Move me emotionally? Yes. Make me feel sad or hopeless? No, thank you. I am careful about what I read and what I expose myself to. I limit my exposure to the news in that I never watch it, I try not to notice the awful headlines that almost leap out of my computer at me, and I try to stay positive and walk on the sunny side of the street. One of the nicest compliments my husband gave me recently is when he told me, "You are charmingly, endearingly, and annoyingly positive." I remind him of this at opportune moments, much to his chagrin.

So what was the important point in this part of my ramble so far? That I'm a writer and I have been aware of my feelings from an early age. That, and I started to decide how I wanted to feel pretty early in my life. I chose what I wanted to pay attention to and I wanted to be happy. In looking back at how this all came together, I can see where the awareness of and intention about feelings is important.

On to the next part. When I was working on pulling this part of the book together, I was thrilled to find the notecards I had jotted my first ideas on. On the first one, bright orange, it reads: "11.14.13 Woke up thinking about my book. It was already published. Don't know what it was about, only that it was complete." Farther down on the card I wrote:

"On the way to work thought about Miracle on 34th Street. That was all about the Law of Attraction. Christmas book about stories and Law of Attraction?"

Under this card is a bright yellow one. On it I wrote:

Wanting/ask   Belief
Anticipation   ^Vibe   Actualization

Rita . . . Is your daughter still horse crazy?
I have a horse I want to give her.

Here, with these two cards, I can see where I was starting to percolate. Above are the pieces of the Law of Attraction. And the Rita/horse note? Proof of where the Law of Attraction had showed up in my life long before I knew what was going on.

I've already mentioned my love of horses. Fortunately, my love of horses was supported by my mom, who, after listening to me beg for riding lessons, finally gave in and let me start riding when I was 6. She made me beg for about a year because she wanted to make sure the passion was mine, and not just a reflection of hers as she had grown up loving horses, too. She had been in love with the milkman's horse and fed him carrots everyday (the horse, not the milkman). She read every one of The Black Stallion books. When I was a kid, she would buy them and read them again before she wrapped them up and gave them to me.

I loved Saturdays as that was the day I got to go to the barn. I got to breathe in the beautiful smell of those gorgeous beasts as my dream came true every week and I learned to ride. I read about horses, I wrote about horses, I dreamed about horses, and I drew pictures of where I would live and what the barn would look like when I had horses. Barns I could draw, horses I drew with my words and my imagination. When I played, I pretended to ride or I galloped around and became the horse itself. Snorting, whinnying, pawing, and jumping. I could do it all. I learned that girly hair toss at an early age because to me it was a horse thing. I remember being called something really creative like "horse girl" a time or two in elementary school, but didn't hear a lot of that. Probably because I took it as a compliment. I was completely, totally in love with horses. I think you get the point and I don't want to bore you. So why is this part important?

Because on a magical day in 1972, when I was ten, on August the 23rd at about 7:30 pm to be exact, my mom's friend, Rita Walby, who has now been elevated to a goddess in my world, GAVE me my very first horse. My mom still remembers the phone call she received one day when Rita asked, "Is your daughter still horse crazy?" Of course my mother had to respond in the affirmative as I was certifiably horse crazy. "I have a horse I want to give her," Rita said. My mother schemed with Rita to surprise me with the best gift ever and that wonderful Wednesday summer night was absolute, pure magic. There I was, a kid who lived in southwest Detroit, now staring into the beautiful brown eyes of her very own four-year-old Quarter Horse, Star Rita. Dreams do come true and now I had proof. I loved her to the moon and back and could fill another book with stories about our adventures, but that really would be another book. My love for horses continues and I still haven't outgrown it. There are three of them munching hay outside even as I type.

So, what was the point of this part of the ramble? That I had all the pieces of LOA the pros say need to be present to manifest: desire, belief, anticipation, the feeling of what I wanted, and the surety that it will happen. I wasn't sure when, but I was absolutely, positively sure that there was a horse in my future. Another important factor that was present was that I had no concern whatsoever about the how. I just KNEW it would happen someday. And probably the most important ingredient I had in excess was the FEELING OF HAVING. That's what they mean when they talk about matching your vibration to what you want. I had those emotions down pat: the feel of the wind whipping through my hair while I rode, the warmth of my horse's skin under my hand, a full movie reel in my head of all the fantastic things we would do together, and the absolute love and joy I had for my horse. All she had to do was show up and step into my life. I was ready.

My yellow card scribbles show that I was pulling together the elements of the LOA and the proof that I had made it happen in my life once before.

On my next card, pink again, I have filled the card with LOA instructions that I think came from Carl Harvey of *The Big Life* and *The Abundance Book Club*. The Law of Attraction is not a secret, but it is rather like a recipe where the ingredients are the same, but how you put it together affects your outcome:

Always tell the best story possible.
Focus on the <u>feelings</u> you want.
Meditate for at least 15 minutes each day.
Still your mind as often as possible.
Feel gratitude as often as possible.
Create and celebrate success.
*CLEAR INTENTION + EXPECTATION (EMOTION BRINGS IT) + ACTION = LOA

I was trying to suck up everything I could get my hands on about creating abundance because, for the first time, I was carrying the full financial responsibility for my family and I was scared. We had moved to Oregon in July of 2012 because I accepted a job offer. My husband supported us moving to Oregon without having seen the area except on our drive through while on our honeymoon 10 years earlier. My daughter wasn't happy about leaving our family and friends and while she settled in well, I still worried about what I had done to my family. My husband's way of making a living just didn't exist in our new location, either. He's a boat guy and had a thriving business in Michigan where we were surrounded by the Great Lakes. He had been shipping boat parts all over the world, but here in Oregon the game had changed. We decided it was best for him to be spending time with our daughter and they explored the glorious wilderness together that is just outside our door here. They went swimming, boating, hiking, fishing, and exploring while I got started with my new job. For the first time in my life, I got to know what real anxiety felt like. Ugh.

At this point I was checking my bank balance every morning with my heart in my throat, praying that nothing had bounced that day. I was also learning that the fear and the anxiety could not be my focus or I was going to keep getting more of that, so I switched to gratitude. I started expressing my gratitude out loud, and with feeling, being grateful if I was in the positive column, even if by pennies.

And then I decided to start writing, my way of creating. Call them what you wish: proclamations, declarations, affirmations, whatever. I wrote them down every morning, and then I would read them out loud to myself, and with feeling. I would let myself marinate in all those good feelings about money. Feelings which were definitely not based on my reality at the time. Then I would just sit for a minute and hold them, eyes shut, cards pressed against my heart, sending my vibes out to whomever was listening. Rather silly, now that I read this, as the person who needed to hear this the most was me.

My cards were filled with 14 (no magic number there, but interesting that I started on the 14th and had 14) different proclamations about my positive relationship with money. Talk about a fantasy. What I was very careful to do was to write out only statements that I could feel good about because they were true. I remember playing around with affirmations before and they always felt silly because they were so far from my current situation I couldn't get behind them and they were cookie cutter statements that just felt phony. Too *Saturday Night Live* Stuart Smalley-ish, by golly. When I started writing these, I was motivated by real financial fear and scarcity. I was starting to really pay attention to the LOA stuff and try and figure it out. I knew my belief and how I felt about every word was important. I had to be able to believe it before I could see it, as Wayne Dyer would say. So as weird as this feels, because oddly enough I can be sort of shy sometimes, I will share these beginning statements with you. I am always grateful when I find examples that fit for me, so if this helps you at all, then I am okay with it. In italics after each one is how I felt about it or justified using it as a proclamation.

1.) **Thank you, God, for all of my blessings!**
Yes! I am and always have been seriously grateful for my blessings.

2.) **I love how it feels to have plenty of money!**
Yes! I may not have "plenty" at the moment, but I knew what it felt like to have money and it feels good.

3.) **I give myself permission to be as rich as I want.** *Yes! I could feel some resistance to this, but I kept this anyway. It got better as time passed. This sounds like I may have gotten it from Denise Duffield Thomas who wrote Get Rich, Lucky Bitch! If so, thanks, Denise!*

4.) **I always have more than enough money.**
This was technically true. We had enough food, we had shelter, and I had a job.

5.) **Money always comes to me with perfect timing.** *Astonishingly true. I have had plenty of just under the wire moments when money would show up and save the day. Insert gratitude here; see proclamation #1.*

6.) **I appreciate money for the good it can do and the things it provides.** *Yes times a million.*

7.) **Every day, my belief in abundance grows.** *Yes! This became more and more true for me, and it is still growing.*

8.) **The Universe can deliver anything I ask for.** *Well, duh. Of course it can. Even though I have sometimes wondered if the Universe lost my address.*

9.) **I know that more money is coming to me now.** *Yes. I did know it. I really did believe this. See delivery concerns above.*

10.) **Money comes to me in fun and unexpected ways now.** *Yes. And it would. I would find little bits of money in weird spots. Sidewalks, cars, pockets, envelopes I was sure were empty, and purses I was sure I cleaned out. I have also received random checks in the mail that seemed to come from nowhere.*

11.) **I love winning money! It is so much fun!** *Yes! It sure is! It doesn't happen to me often, but it sure is fun.*

12.) **The Universe always provides me with everything I need.** *Yes! Here I am and I'm okay.*

13.) **I love money and magnetically draw it to me now.** *Yes! I would bless every little penny I found and I would talk to it like it was my best friend and the biggest treasure ever. I am sure I looked quite dotty to anyone who saw me. I still exclaim over every penny and thank it for coming to me. I now find dimes and quarters more often than I find pennies.*

14.) **I love how free I am to give to others because I now and always have money.** *Yes! This one is the best! I always try to give something. My grandmother, who lived on a small, fixed income, would always give something to those outside stores or on a corner and say, "No matter how badly off you may think you are, there is always someone who is more in need than you are." Thank you, Grandma, for showing me your generous heart and setting a great example.*

I have come to realize that this is what it means to raise your vibration. Your vibe has to match what it is you are trying to create, so you can't create from feelings of lack. It took me quite a while to "get" this as I can be quite literal when it comes to words. When I heard Paul Scheele's words, "You attract to you whatever is similar in vibration" I remember thinking "What the heck does that mean??? I would like a new horse trailer. Am I supposed to figure out what a horse trailer vibes like? And where would I learn THAT?" I later figured out that it is the feeling that you energetically express when you can mentally experience what it's like to HAVE what you desire.

I filled the cards front and back and while I didn't write every single day I continued until July of 2014. Did I stop because I came into a fortune? No. But somewhere along the line the financial death-grip loosened. Things got better, and I started to have an improved relationship with money. I read books (a lot of books), I did some tapping (I highly recommend this), worked on my belief system and mindset (still doing that), and the tide started to turn. I started meditating and with the help of Dr. Joe Dispenza's guided meditations I actually stepped into the Quantum Field for the first time on November 10th, 2014. During that glorious and cosmic connection I really felt that abundance was in me. It came to me that I was abundance, and I didn't have to keep looking for it outside of myself. That very day I received a check in the mail for more than $1, 200.00, which felt like an absolute fortune to me. It still does.

The following spring I had an amazing opportunity: my agency gathered a bunch of us together and offered us a chance to go away to camp. Okay, so not camp, but the Columbia Leadership Institute. An intensive training in leadership at the exclusive Skamania Lodge? Count me in! I leapt at the opportunity and was the first in the group to volunteer. This stuff was right up my alley and I loved it. At the end of our second week we had a closing ceremony and each team had to put on a performance/presentation of some sort. We put our heads together and tried to come up with something. And out it came . . . rhyming comes easily to me and so I started writing about our shenanigans and what we had learned over the course of our training. The rest of the team scrambled to make up a skit to match my words and our irreverent presentation was a hit. What was interesting about this was that as I read out the poem to our audience, I was covered in goose bumps. It was oddly reminiscent of *The Night Before Christmas*, even though I didn't notice that while I was writing it. And after I was done one of my colleagues jokingly asked if I would come to his house every Christmas Eve and read to his kids.

My next notes start with: "On the way to work." I get so many of my ideas while I am driving or while I am in the shower. My scribbles go on from there and the first two pages are jots about different aspects I wanted to include. And then on page three of my notes I started writing the poem that would become this book. It flowed pretty easily once I got started. My husband suggested the part about Santas being everywhere and how Santa's magic gets used where there is the greatest need. He and my daughter cheered me on and listened over and over as I read it to them.

While I am not much of a cook, this poem is my recipe for life. Santa reminds our protagonist that she has always known how to make the magic happen in her life, she has just forgotten as she has "been older too long." All the ingredients that the experts say you need to make things happen in your life are there: knowing what you want, writing it out, setting your intention right down to the last little detail, feeling the joy of having it, the rock solid expectation of knowing it's

coming, seeing it, believing it, taking action, and forgetting about the how. As children, we don't let "reality" get in the way of us deciding whether or not we are going to get something. We know what we want and we go after it the way we know how. We ask Santa for it.

I believe that Santa and God and the Universe and Spirit and whomever else you would like to toss in there are all working together on our behalf. I believe every word of what I have written. I have lived it, the good and the bad. I still have to remind myself that the magic is in me. It is my connection to the Divine. It is in each and every one of us. We have the ability to create the lives we dream about. When we focus on the feelings of love, joy, and gratitude and take action, the magic happens.

And I still believe in Santa Claus. Do you?

For Your Perusal. . .

Ask and It Is Given: Learning to Manifest Your Desires, by Esther and Jerry Hicks

Becoming Supernatural: How Common People Are Doing the Uncommon, by Dr. Joe Dispenza

The Biology of Belief: Unleashing the Power of Consciousness, Matter, & Miracles, by Bruce Lipton, PhD.

The Course in Manifesting, by Genevieve Davis

E-Squared: Nine Do-It-Yourself Energy Experiments That Prove Your Thoughts Create Your Reality, by Pam Grout

Get Rich, Lucky Bitch!: Release Your Money Blocks and Live a First-Class Life, by Denise Duffield Thomas

The Magic, by Rhonda Byrne

The Magical Path: Creating the Life of Your Dreams and a World That Works for All, by Marc Allen

Mind to Matter: The Astonishing Science of How Your Brain Creates Material Reality, by Dawson Church

Money, A Love Story, by Kate Northrup

Quantum Enigma: Physics Encounters Consciousness, by Bruce Rosenblum & Fred Kuttner

The Seven Spiritual Laws of Success, by Deepak Chopra

The Tapping Solution: A Revolutionary System for Stress-Free Living, by Nick Ortner

Think and Grow Rich, by Napoleon Hill

Think and Grow Rich for Women: Using Your Power to Create Success and Significance, by Sharon Lechter

You2: A High Velocity Formula for Multiplying Your Personal Effectiveness in Quantum Leaps, By Price Pritchett

You Are a Badass: How to Stop Doubting Your Greatness and Start Living an Awesome Life, by Jen Sincero

You Were Born Rich, by Bob Proctor

Printed in the United States
By Bookmasters